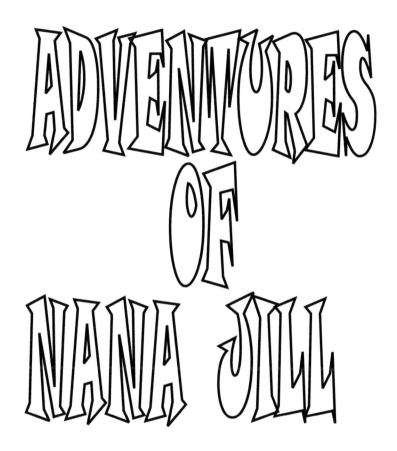

ADVENTURES OF NANA JILL

(At the Bakery)

BY JANE FRANCES

ILLUSTRATED BY IKE FRANCIS

ADVENTURES OF NANA JILL

BY JANE FRANCES, ILLUSTRATED BY IKE FRANCIS

Order this book online at www.trafford.com
or email orders@trafford.com

Most Trafford titles are also available at major online book retailers.

Print information available on the last page.

ISBN: 978-1-4907-7621-7 (sc)
      978-1-4907-7620-0 (e)

Our mission is to efficiently provide the world's finest, most comprehensive book publishing service, enabling every author to experience success. To find out how to publish your book, your way, and have it available worldwide, visit us online at www.trafford.com

Trafford rev. 08/19/2016

 www.trafford.com

North America & international
toll-free: 1 888 232 4444 (USA & Canada)
phone: 250 383 6864 ♦ fax: 812 355 4082

There goes Nana Jill,
hobbling down the hill.
She has her cane in hand while leading her little cat, Milly on a leash.
Milly shuffled alongside Nana Jill, wishing it was a dog.

1

In goes Nana Jill into her old bakery.
She was hoping to purchase a fresh loaf and chat with
her old friend, Olaf, the baker at the bakery.

2

Behind Nana Jill, came an intruder, prepared to pilfer.
He marched straight to the counter, demanding for cash
and threatening to harm Olaf and his staff.

3

Quickly goes Nana Jill into action.
She swung her stick at the intruder's head, knocking him down.
"Awhhhh!", snickered the surprised intruder as
he fell to the floor.

4

He had not expected such force and strength from an
old lady, who'd surprisingly knocked him out.
He whimpered and begged for mercy.
Nana Jill pinned him down with her stick and was ready to take another swing.

As soon as he was able to scramble back on his feet, off ran the oaf.

Neither with a loaf

Nor any cash.

He sped off as fast as he could to evade the wrath of Nana Jill

The guard gave a chase, trying to apprehend the thief.
He was unable to catch him, though, after the thief ran
into a crowd and seemingly disappeared.

Olaf and his staff were grateful for Nana Jill's help.
They hugged and thanked her profusely for her help.
They declined to accept payment for her loaf and gave her an extra one.

Nana Jill soon departed with her cat in tow.
They headed home, walking cheerily up the hill. They were also laden with
the two loafs that she had received from Olaf in appreciation for her help.

9

Later that evening, Nana Jill sat in her porch.
She was ready to relax and enjoy a good old cup of tea and a slice of bun.
It was a wonderful end to an eventful day.

Color me

Color me

Color me

Color me

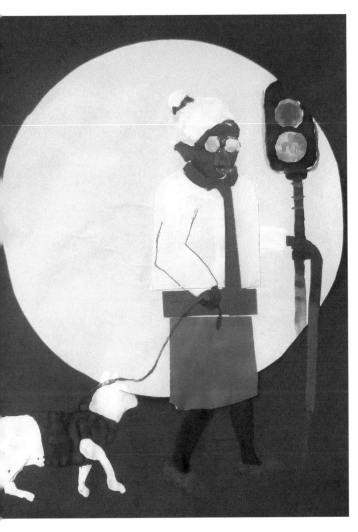

The Adventures of Nana Jill

(AT THE BAKERY)

By

JANE FRANCES

ILLUSTRATED BY

IKE FRANCIS

Printed in the United States
By Bookmasters